This edition published by Parragon in 2013

Parragon
Chartist House
15-17 Trim Street
Bath BA1 1HA, UK
www.parragon.com

Printed in China

Goodnight Little One

Parragon
Bath • New York • Singapore • Hong Kong • Cologne • Delhi
Melbourne • Amsterdam • Johannesburg • Shenzhen

Little donkey on the hill,
Standing there so very still.

Making faces at the skies,

Little donkey
close *your* eyes.

Little monkey in the tree,
Swinging there so merrily.
Throwing coconuts at the skies,

Little monkey
close your eyes.

Silly sheep that slowly crop,
Night has come and you must stop,

Chewing grass beneath the skies,
Silly sheep now close *your* eyes.

Little pig that squeals about,
Make no noises with your snout.

No more squealing to the skies,

Little pig now
close *your* eyes.

Wild young birds that sweetly sing,
Curve your heads beneath your wing.
Dark night covers all the skies,
Wild young birds now close *your* eyes.

Old black cat down in the barn,
Keeping five small kittens warm.
Let the wind blow in the skies,

Dear old black cat
close *your* eyes.

Little child all tucked in bed,
Looking such a sleepyhead.
Stars are quiet in the skies,

Little child now
close *your* eyes.